D0443155

THE POST OFFICE

THE MACMILLAN COMPANY
NEW YORK · BOSTON · CHICAGO · DALLAS
ATLANTA · SAN FRANCISCO

MACMILLAN & CO., LIMITED
LONDON · BOMBAY · CALCUTTA
MELBOURNE

THE MACMILLAN CO. OF CANADA, LTD.
TORONTO

THE POST OFFICE

BY

RABINDRANATH TAGORE

///

New York
THE MACMILLAN COMPANY
1914

DRAMATIS PERSONÆ

MADHAV
AMAL, his adopted child
SUDHA, a little flower girl
THE DOCTOR
DAIRYMAN
WATCHMAN
GAFFER
VILLAGE HEADMAN, a bully
KING'S HERALD
ROYAL PHYSICIAN

THE POST OFFICE

ACT I

THE POST OFFICE

ACT I

[*Madhav's House*]

Madhav

What a state I am in! Before he
came, nothing mattered; I felt so free.
But now that he has come, goodness
knows from where, my heart is filled
with his dear self, and my home will
be no home to me when he leaves.
Doctor, do you think he——

Physician

If there's life in his fate, then he will
live long. But what the medical scriptures say, it seems——

Madhav

Great heavens, what?

Physician

The scriptures have it: "Bile or palsey, cold or gout spring all alike."

Madhav

Oh, get along, don't fling your scriptures at me; you only make me more anxious; tell me what I can do.

Physician [Taking snuff]

The patient needs the most scrupulous care.

Madhav

That's true; but tell me how.

Physician

I have already mentioned, on no account must he be let out of doors.

Madhav

Poor child, it is very hard to keep him indoors all day long.

Physician

What else can you do? The autumn sun and the damp are both very bad for the little fellow—for the scriptures have it:

"In wheezing, swoon or in nervous fret,
  In jaundice or leaden eyes——"

Madhav

Never mind the scriptures, please. Eh, then we must shut the poor thing up. Is there no other method?

Physician

None at all: for, "In the wind and in the sun——"

Madhav

What will your "in this and in that" do for me now? Why don't you let them alone and come straight to the point? What's to be done then? Your system is very, very hard for the poor boy; and he is so quiet too with all his

pain and sickness. It tears my heart to
see him wince, as he takes your medicine.

Physician

The more he winces, the surer is the
effect. That's why the sage Chyabana
observes: "In medicine as in good ad-
vices, the least palatable ones are the
truest." Ah, well! I must be trotting
now. [*Exit*]

[*Gaffer enters*]

Madhav

Well, I'm jiggered, there's Gaffer
now.

Gaffer

Why, why, I won't bite you.

Madhav

No, but you are a devil to send children off their heads.

Gaffer

But you aren't a child, and you've no child in the house; why worry then?

Madhav

Oh, but I have brought a child into the house.

Gaffer

Indeed, how so?

Madhav

You remember how my wife was dying to adopt a child?

Gaffer

Yes, but that's an old story; you didn't like the idea.

Madhav

You know, brother, how hard all this getting money in has been. That somebody else's child would sail in and

waste all this money earned with so
much trouble—Oh, I hated the idea.
But this boy clings to my heart in
such a queer sort of way——

Gaffer

So that's the trouble! and your
money goes all for him and feels jolly
lucky it does go at all.

Madhav

Formerly, earning was a sort of pas-
sion with me; I simply couldn't help
working for money. Now, I make
money and as I know it is all for this
dear boy, earning becomes a joy to me.

Gaffer

Ah, well, and where did you pick him
up?

Madhav

He is the son of a man who was a
brother to my wife by village ties. He

has had no mother since infancy; and now the other day he lost his father as well.

Gaffer

Poor thing: and so he needs me all the more.

Madhav

The doctor says all the organs of his little body are at loggerheads with each other, and there isn't much hope for his life. There is only one way to save him and that is to keep him out of this autumn wind and sun. But you are such a terror! What with this game of yours at your age, too, to get children out of doors!

Gaffer

God bless my soul! So I'm already as bad as autumn wind and sun, eh! But, friend, I know something, too, of the game of keeping them indoors. When my day's work is over I am com-

ing in to make friends with this child
of yours.　[*Exit*]

[*Amal enters*]

Amal

Uncle, I say, Uncle!

Madhav

Hullo!　Is that you, Amal?

Amal

Mayn't I be out of the courtyard at
all?

Madhav

No, my dear, no.

Amal

See, there where Auntie grinds lentils
in the quirn, the squirrel is sitting with
his tail up and with his wee hands he's
picking up the broken grains of lentils

and crunching them. Can't I run up there?

Madhav

No, my darling, no.

Amal

Wish I were a squirrel!—it would be lovely. Uncle, why won't you let me go about?

Madhav

Doctor says it's bad for you to be out.

Amal

How can the doctor know?

Madhav

What a thing to say! The doctor can't know and he reads such huge books!

Amal

Does his book-learning tell him everything?

Madhav

Of course, don't you know!

Amal [*With a sigh*]

Ah, I am so stupid! I don't read books.

Madhav

Now, think of it; very, very learned people are all like you; they are never out of doors.

Amal

Aren't they really?

Madhav

No, how can they? Early and late they toil and moil at their books, and they've eyes for nothing else. Now, my little man, you are going to be learned when you grow up; and then you will stay at home and read such big books, and people will notice you and say, "he's a wonder."

Amal

No, no, Uncle; I beg of you by your dear feet—I don't want to be learned, I won't.

Madhav

Dear, dear; it would have been my saving if I could have been learned.

Amal

No, I would rather go about and see everything that there is.

Madhav

Listen to that! See! What will you see, what is there so much to see?

Amal

See that far-away hill from our window—I often long to go beyond those hills and right away.

Madhav

Oh, you silly! As if there's nothing more to be done but just get up to the top of that hill and away! Eh! You don't talk sense, my boy. Now listen, since that hill stands there upright as a barrier, it means you can't get beyond it. Else, what was the use in heaping up so many large stones to make such a big affair of it, eh!

Amal

Uncle, do you think it is meant to prevent your crossing over? It seems to me because the earth can't speak it raises its hands into the sky and beckons. And those who live far and sit alone by their windows can see

the signal.   But I suppose the learned
people——

Madhav

No, they don't have time for that
sort of nonsense.   They are not crazy
like you.

Amal

Do you know, yesterday I met someone quite as crazy as I am.

Madhav

Gracious me, really, how so?

Amal

He had a bamboo staff on his shoulder with a small bundle at the top, and
a brass pot in his left hand, and an old
pair of shoes on; he was making for
those hills straight across that meadow
there.   I called out to him and asked,
"Where are you going?"   He answered,

"I don't know, anywhere!" I asked
again, "Why are you going?" He
said, "I'm going out to seek work."
Say, Uncle, have you to seek work?

Madhav

Of course I have to. There's many
about looking for jobs.

Amal

How lovely! I'll go about, like them
too, finding things to do.

Madhav

Suppose you seek and don't find.
Then——

Amal

Wouldn't that be jolly? Then I
should go farther! I watched that man
slowly walking on with his pair of worn
out shoes. And when he got to where
the water flows under the fig tree, he

stopped and washed his feet in the stream. Then he took out from his bundle some gram-flour, moistened it with water and began to eat. Then he tied up his bundle and shouldered it again; tucked up his cloth above his knees and crossed the stream. I've asked Auntie to let me go up to the stream, and eat my gram-flour just like him.

Madhav

And what did your Auntie say to that?

Amal

Auntie said, "Get well and then I'll take you over there." Please, Uncle, when shall I get well?

Madhav

It won't be long, dear.

Amal

Really, but then I shall go right away the moment I'm well again.

Madhav

And where will you go?

Amal

Oh, I will walk on, crossing so many streams, wading through water. Everybody will be asleep with their doors shut in the heat of the day and I will tramp on and on seeking work far, very far.

Madhav

I see! I think you had better be getting well first; then——

Amal

But then you won't want me to be learned, will you, Uncle?

Madhav

What would you rather be then?

Amal

I can't think of anything just now;
but I'll tell you later on.

Madhav

Very well.   But mind you, you
aren't to call out and talk to strangers
again.

Amal

But I love to talk to strangers!

Madhav

Suppose they had kidnapped you?

Amal

That would have been splendid!
But no one ever takes me away. They
all want me to stay in here.

Madhav

I am off to my work—but, darling, you won't go out, will you?

Amal

No, I won't. But, Uncle, you'll let me be in this room by the roadside.

[*Exit Madhav*]

Dairyman

Curds, curds, good nice curds.

Amal

Curdseller, I say, Curdseller.

Dairyman

Why do you call me? Will you buy some curds?

Amal

How can I buy? I have no money.

Dairyman

What a boy! Why call out then?
Ugh! What a waste of time.

Amal

I would go with you if I could.

Dairyman

With me?

Amal

Yes, I seem to feel homesick when I
hear you call from far down the road.

Dairyman [*Lowering his yoke-pole*]
Whatever are you doing here, my
child?

Amal

The doctor says I'm not to be out,
so I sit here all day long.

Dairyman

My poor child, whatever has happened to you?

Amal

I can't tell. You see I am not learned, so I don't know what's the matter with me. Say, Dairyman, where do you come from?

Dairyman

From our village.

Amal

Your village? Is it very far?

Dairyman

Our village lies on the river Shamli at the foot of the Panch-mura hills.

Amal

Panch-mura hills! Shamli river! I wonder. I may have seen your village. I can't think when though!

Dairyman

Have you seen it? Been to the foot of those hills?

Amal

Never. But I seem to remember having seen it. Your village is under some very old big trees, just by the side of the red road—isn't that so?

Dairyman

That's right, child.

Amal

And on the slope of the hill cattle grazing.

Dairyman

How wonderful! Aren't there cattle grazing in our village! Indeed, there are!

Amal

And your women with red sarees fill
their pitchers from the river and carry
them on their heads.

Dairyman

Good, that's right. Women from
our dairy village do come and draw
their water from the river; but then it
isn't everyone who has a red saree to
put on. But, my dear child, surely
you must have been there for a walk
some time.

Amal

Really, Dairyman, never been there
at all. But the first day doctor lets
me go out, you are going to take me
to your village.

Dairyman

I will, my child, with pleasure.

Amal

And you'll teach me to cry curds
and shoulder the yoke like you and
walk the long, long road?

Dairyman

Dear, dear, did you ever? Why
should you sell curds? No, you will
read big books and be learned.

Amal

No, I never want to be learned—I'll
be like you and take my curds from the
village by the red road near the old
banyan tree, and I will hawk it from
cottage to cottage. Oh, how do you
cry—"Curd, curd, good nice curd!"
Teach me the tune, will you?

Dairyman

Dear, dear, teach you the tune; what
an idea!

Amal

Please do. I love to hear it. I can't tell you how queer I feel when I hear you cry out from the bend of that road, through the line of those trees! Do you know I feel like that when I hear the shrill cry of kites from almost the end of the sky?

Dairyman

Dear child, will you have some curds? Yes, do.

Amal

But I have no money.

Dairyman

No, no, no, don't talk of money! You'll make me so happy if you have a little curds from me.

Amal

Say, have I kept you too long?

Dairyman

Not a bit; it has been no loss to me at all; you have taught me how to be happy selling curds. [*Exit*]

Amal [*Intoning*]

Curds, curds, good nice curds—from the dairy village—from the country of the Panch-mura hills by the Shamli bank. Curds, good curds; in the early morning the women make the cows stand in a row under the trees and milk them, and in the evening they turn the milk into curds. Curds, good curds. Hello, there's the watchman on his rounds. Watchman, I say, come and have a word with me.

Watchman

What's all this row you are making? Aren't you afraid of the likes of me?

Amal

No, why should I be?

Watchman

Suppose I march you off then?

Amal

Where will you take me to? Is it very far, right beyond the hills?

Watchman

Suppose I march you straight to the King?

Amal

To the King! Do, will you? But the doctor won't let me go out. No one can ever take me away. I've got to stay here all day long.

Watchman

Doctor won't let you, poor fellow! So I see! Your face is pale and there are dark rings round your eyes. Your veins stick out from your poor thin hands.

Amal

Won't you sound the gong, Watchman?

Watchman

Time has not yet come.

Amal

How curious! Some say time has not yet come, and some say time has gone by! But surely your time will come the moment you strike the gong!

Watchman

That's not possible; I strike up the gong only when it is time.

Amal

Yes, I love to hear your gong. When it is midday and our meal is over, Uncle goes off to his work and Auntie falls asleep reading her Rāmayana, and in the courtyard under the shadow of the wall our doggie sleeps with his nose in his curled up tail; then your gong strikes out, "Dong, dong, dong!" Tell me why does your gong sound?

Watchman

My gong sounds to tell the people, Time waits for none, but goes on for-ever.

Amal

Where, to what land?

Watchman

That none knows.

Amal

Then I suppose no one has ever been there! Oh, I do wish to fly with the time to that land of which no one knows anything.

Watchman

All of us have to get there one day, my child.

Amal

Have I too?

Watchman

Yes, you too!

Amal

But doctor won't let me out.

Watchman

One day the doctor himself may take you there by the hand.

Amal

He won't; you don't know him. He only keeps me in.

Watchman

One greater than he comes and lets us free.

Amal

When will this great doctor come for me? I can't stick in here any more.

Watchman

Shouldn't talk like that, my child.

Amal

No. I am here where they have left me—I never move a bit. But when your gong goes off, dong, dong, dong, it goes to my heart. Say, Watchman?

Watchman

Yes, my dear.

Amal

Say, what's going on there in that big house on the other side, where there is a flag flying high up and the people are always going in and out?

Watchman

Oh, there?   That's our new Post Office.

Amal

Post Office?   Whose?

Watchman

Whose?   Why, the King's surely!

Amal

Do letters come from the King to his office here?

Watchman

Of course.   One fine day there may be a letter for you in there.

Amal

A letter for me?   But I am only a little boy.

Watchman

The King sends tiny notes to little boys.

Amal

Oh, how lovely! When shall I have my letter? How do you guess he'll write to me?

Watchman

Otherwise why should he set his Post Office here right in front of your open window, with the golden flag flying?

Amal

But who will fetch me my King's letter when it comes?

Watchman

The King has many postmen. Don't you see them run about with round gilt badges on their chests?

Amal

Well, where do they go?

Watchman

Oh, from door to door, all through the country.

Amal

I'll be the King's postman when I grow up.

Watchman

Ha! ha! Postman, indeed! Rain or shine, rich or poor, from house to house delivering letters—that's very great work!

Amal

That's what I'd like best. What makes you smile so? Oh, yes, your work is great too. When it is silent everywhere in the heat of the noonday, your gong sounds, Dong, dong, dong,— and sometimes when I wake up at night all of a sudden and find our lamp blown out, I can hear through the darkness your gong slowly sounding, Dong, dong, dong!

Watchman

There's the village headman! I must be off. If he catches me gossiping with you there'll be a great to do.

Amal

The headman? Whereabouts is he?

Watchman

Right down the road there; see that huge palm-leaf umbrella hopping along? That's him!

Amal

I suppose the King's made him our headman here?

Watchman

Made him? Oh, no! A fussy busy-body! He knows so many ways of making himself unpleasant that everybody is afraid of him. It's just a game for the likes of him, making trouble for everybody. I must be off now! Mustn't keep work waiting, you know! I'll drop in again to-morrow morning and tell you all the news of the town. [*Exit*]

Amal

It would be splendid to have a letter from the King every day. I'll read them at the window. But, oh! I can't read writing. Who'll read them out to me, I wonder! Auntie reads her Rāmayana; she may know the King's writing. If no one will, then I must keep them carefully and read them when I'm grown up. But if the postman can't find me? Headman, Mr. Headman, may I have a word with you?

Headman

Who is yelling after me on the high-way? Oh, you wretched monkey!

Amal

You're the headman. Everybody minds you.

Headman [*Looking pleased*]

Yes, oh yes, they do! They must!

Amal

Do the King's postmen listen to you?

Headman

They've got to. By Jove, I'd like to see——

Amal

Will you tell the postman it's Amal who sits by the window here?

Headman

What's the good of that?

Amal

In case there's a letter for me.

Headman

A letter for you! Whoever's going to write to you?

Amal

If the King does.

Headman

Ha! ha! What an uncommon little fellow you are! Ha! ha! the King indeed, aren't you his bosom friend, eh! You haven't met for a long while and the King is pining, I am sure. Wait till to-morrow and you'll have your letter.

Amal

Say, Headman, why do you speak to me in that tone of voice? Are you cross?

Headman

Upon my word! Cross, indeed! You write to the King! Madhav is devilish swell nowadays. He'd made a little pile; and so kings and padishahs are everyday talk with his people. Let me find him once and I'll make him dance. Oh, you snipper-snapper! I'll get the King's letter sent to your house —indeed I will!

Amal

No, no, please don't trouble yourself about it.

Headman

And why not, pray! I'll tell the King about you and he won't be very

long. One of his footmen will come
along presently for news of you. Madhav's impudence staggers me. If the
King hears of this, that'll take some
of his nonsense out of him. [*Exit*]

Amal

Who are you walking there? How
your anklets tinkle! Do stop a while,
dear, won't you?

[*A Girl enters*]

Girl

I haven't a moment to spare; it is
already late!

Amal

I see, you don't wish to stop; I don't
care to stay on here either.

Girl

You make me think of some late star
of the morning! Whatever's the matter
with you?

Amal

I don't know; the doctor won't let
me out.

Girl

Ah me! Don't then! Should listen
to the doctor. People'll be cross with
you if you're naughty. I know, always
looking out and watching must make
you feel tired. Let me close the window a bit for you.

Amal

No, don't, only this one's open! All
the others are shut. But will you tell
me who you are? Don't seem to know
you.

Girl

I am Sudha.

Amal

What Sudha?

Sudha

Don't you know? Daughter of the flower-seller here.

Amal

What do *you* do?

Sudha

I gather flowers in my basket.

Amal

Oh, flower gathering! That is why your feet seem so glad and your anklets jingle so merrily as you walk. Wish I could be out too. Then I would pick some flowers for you from the very topmost branches right out of sight.

Sudha

Would you really? Do you know more about flowers than I?

Amal

Yes, I *do*, quite as much. I know all about Champa of the fairy tale and his seven brothers. If only they let me, I'll go right into the dense forest where you can't find your way. And where the honey-sipping humming-bird rocks himself on the end of the thinnest branch, I will flower out as a champa. Would you be my sister Parul?

Sudha

You are silly! How can I be sister Parul when I am Sudha and my mother is Sasi, the flower-seller? I have to weave so many garlands a day. It would be jolly if I could lounge here like you!

Amal

What would you do then, all the day long?

Sudha

I could have great times with my doll Benay the bride, and Meni the pussy-cat and—but I say it is getting late and I mustn't stop, or I won't find a single flower.

Amal

Oh, wait a little longer; I do like it so!

Sudha

Ah, well—now don't you be naughty. Be good and sit still and on my way back home with the flowers I'll come and talk with you.

Amal

And you'll let me have a flower then?

Sudha

No, how can I? It has to be **paid** for.

Amal

I'll pay when I grow up—before I leave to look for work out on the other side of that stream there.

Sudha

Very well, then.

Amal

And you'll come back when you have your flowers?

Sudha

I will.

Amal

You will, really?

Sudha

Yes, I will.

Amal

You won't forget me? I am Amal,
remember that.

Sudha

I won't forget you, you'll see. [*Exit*]

[*A Troop of Boys enter*]

Amal

Say, brothers, where are you all off
to? Stop here a little.

Boys

We're off to play.

Amal

What will you play at, brothers?

Boys

We'll play at being ploughmen.

First Boy [*Showing a stick*]

This is our ploughshare.

Second Boy

We two are the pair of oxen.

Amal

And you're going to play the whole day?

Boys

Yes, all day long.

Amal

And you'll come back home in the evening by the road along the river bank?

Boys

Yes.

Amal

Do you pass our house on your way home?

Boys

You come out to play with us, yes do.

Amal

Doctor won't let me out.

Boys

Doctor! Suppose the likes of you mind the doctor. Let's be off; it is getting late.

Amal

Don't. Why not play on the road near this window? I could watch you then.

Third Boy

What can we play at here?

Amal

With all these toys of mine lying about. Here you are, have them. I can't play alone. They are getting dirty and are of no use to me.

Boys

How jolly! What fine toys! Look, here's a ship. There's old mother Jatai; say, chaps, ain't he a gorgeous sepoy? And you'll let us have them all? You don't really mind?

Amal

No, not a bit; have them by all means.

Boys

You don't want them back?

Amal

Oh, no, I shan't want them.

Boys

Say, won't you get a scolding for this?

Amal

No one will scold me. But will you play with them in front of our door for a while every morning? I'll get you new ones when these are old.

Boys

Oh, yes, we will. Say, chaps, put these sepoys into a line. We'll play at war; where can we get a musket? Oh, look here, this bit of reed will do nicely. Say, but you're off to sleep already.

Amal

I'm afraid I'm sleepy. I don't know, I feel like it at times. I have been sitting a long while and I'm tired; my back aches.

Boys

It's only early noon now. How is it you're sleepy? Listen! The gong's sounding the first watch.

Amal

Yes, dong, dong, dong, it tolls me
to sleep.

Boys

We had better go then. We'll come
in again to-morrow morning.

Amal

I want to ask you something before
you go. You are always out—do you
know of the King's postmen?

Boys

Yes, quite well.

Amal

Who are they? Tell me their names.

Boys

One's Badal, a n o t h e r ' s Sarat.
There's so many of them.

Amal

Do you think they will know me if there's a letter for me?

Boys

Surely, if your name's on the letter they will find you out.

Amal

When you call in to-morrow morning, will you bring one of them along so that he'll know me?

Boys

Yes, if you like.

CURTAIN

THE POST OFFICE

ACT II

THE POST OFFICE

ACT II

[Amal in Bed]

Amal

Can't I go near the window to-day,
Uncle?   Would the doctor mind that
too?

Madhav

Yes, darling, you see you've made
yourself worse squatting there day after
day.

Amal

Oh, no, I don't know if it's made me
more ill, but I always feel well when
I'm there.

Madhav

No, you don't; you squat there and make friends with the whole lot of people round here, old and young, as if they are holding a fair right under my eaves—flesh and blood won't stand that strain. Just see—your face is quite pale.

Amal

Uncle, I fear my fakir'll pass and not see me by the window.

Madhav

Your fakir, whoever's that?

Amal

He comes and chats to me of the many lands where he's been. I love to hear him.

Madhav

How's that? I don't know of any fakirs.

Amal

This is about the time he comes in. I beg of you, by your dear feet, ask him in for a moment to talk to me here.

[*Gaffer Enters in a Fakir's Guise*]

Amal

There you are. Come here, Fakir, by my bedside.

Madhav

Upon my word, but this is——

Gaffer [*Winking hard*]

I am the fakir.

Madhav

It beats my reckoning what you're not.

Amal

Where have you been this time, Fakir?

Fakir

To the Isle of Parrots. I am just back.

Madhav

The Parrots' Isle!

Fakir

Is it so very astonishing? Am I like you, man? A journey doesn't cost a thing. I tramp just where I like.

Amal [*Clapping*]

How jolly for you! Remember your promise to take me with you as your follower when I'm well.

Fakir

Of course, and I'll teach you such secrets too of travelling that nothing

in sea or forest or mountain can bar
your way.

Madhav

What's all this rigmarole?

Gaffer

Amal, my dear, I bow to nothing in
sea or mountain; but if the doctor joins
in with this uncle of yours, then I with
all my magic must own myself beaten.

Amal

No.   Uncle shan't tell the doctor.
And I promise to lie quiet; but the day
I am well, off I go with the Fakir and
nothing in sea or mountain or torrent
shall stand in my way.

Madhav

Fie, dear child, don't keep on harp-
ing upon going! It makes me so sad
to hear you talk so.

Amal

Tell me, Fakir, what the Parrots' Isle is like.

Gaffer

It's a land of wonders; it's a haunt of birds. There's no man; and they neither speak nor walk, they simply sing and they fly.

Amal

How glorious! And it's by some sea?

Gaffer

Of course. It's on the sea.

Amal

And green hills are there?

Gaffer

Indeed, they live among the green hills; and in the time of the sunset when there is a red glow on the hillside, all the birds with their green wings flock back to their nests.

Amal

And there are waterfalls!

Gaffer

Dear me, of course; you don't have a hill without its waterfalls. Oh, it's like molten diamonds; and, my dear, what dances they have! Don't they make the pebbles sing as they rush over them to the sea. No devil of a doctor can stop them for a moment. The birds looked upon me as nothing but a man, quite a trifling creature without wings—and they would have nothing to do with me. Were it not so I would build a small cabin for my-self among their crowd of nests and pass my days counting the sea waves.

Amal

How I wish I were a bird! Then——

Gaffer

But that would have been a bit of a job; I hear you've fixed up with the dairyman to be a hawker of curds when you grow up; I'm afraid such business won't flourish among birds; you might land yourself into serious loss.

Madhav

Really this is too much. Between you two I shall turn crazy. Now, I'm off.

Amal

Has the dairyman been, Uncle?

Madhav

And why shouldn't he? He won't bother his head running errands for your pet fakir, in and out among the

nests in his Parrots' Isle. But he has
left a jar of curd for you saying that he
is rather busy with his niece's wedding
in the village, and he has got to order
a band at Kamlipara.

Amal

But he is going to marry me to his
little niece.

Gaffer

Dear me, we are in a fix now.

Amal

He said she would find me a lovely
little bride with a pair of pearl drops
in her ears and dressed in a lovely red
sāree; and in the morning she would
milk with her own hands the black cow
and feed me with warm milk with foam
on it from a brand new earthen cruse;
and in the evenings she would carry the
lamp round the cow-house, and then

come and sit by me to tell me tales of Champa and his six brothers.

Gaffer

How delicious! The prospect tempts even me, a hermit! But never mind, dear, about this wedding. Let it be. I tell you when you wed there'll be no lack of nieces in his household.

Madhav

Shut up! This is more than I can stand. [*Exit*]

Amal

Fakir, now that Uncle's off, just tell me, has the King sent me a letter to the Post Office?

Gaffer

I gather that his letter has already started; but it's still on the way.

Amal

On the way? Where is it? Is it on
that road winding through the trees
which you can follow to the end of the
forest when the sky is quite clear
after rain?

Gaffer

That's so. You know all about it
already.

Amal

I do, everything.

Gaffer

So I see, but how?

Amal

I can't say; but it's quite clear to me.
I fancy I've seen it often in days long
gone by. How long ago I can't tell.

Do you know when? I can see it all: there, the King's postman coming down the hillside alone, a lantern in his left hand and on his back a bag of letters; climbing down for ever so long, for days and nights, and where at the foot of the mountain the waterfall becomes a stream he takes to the footpath on the bank and walks on through the rye; then comes the sugarcane field and he disappears into the narrow lane cutting through the tall stems of sugarcanes; then he reaches the open meadow where the cricket chirps and where there is not a single man to be seen, only the snipe wagging their tails and poking at the mud with their bills. I can feel him coming nearer and nearer and my heart becomes glad.

Gaffer

My eyes aren't young; but you make me see all the same.

Amal

Say, Fakir, do you know the King who has this Post Office?

Gaffer

I do; I go to him for my alms every day.

Amal

Good! When I get well, I must have my alms too from him, mayn't I?

Gaffer

You won't need to ask, my dear, he'll give it to you of his own accord.

Amal

No, I would go to his gate and cry, "Victory to thee, O King!" and dancing to the tabor's sound, ask for alms. Won't it be nice?

Gaffer

It would be splendid, and if you're with me, I shall have my full share. But what'll you ask?

Amal

I shall say, "Make me your postman, that I may go about lantern in hand, delivering your letters from door to door. Don't let me stay at home all day!

Gaffer

What is there to be sad for, my child, even were you to stay at home?

Amal

It isn't sad. When they shut me in here first I felt the day was so long. Since the King's Post Office I like it more and more being indoors, and as I think I shall get a letter one day, I feel quite happy and then I don't mind being quiet and alone. I wonder if I shall make out what'll be in the King's letter?

Gaffer

Even if you didn't wouldn't it be enough if it just bore your name?

[*Madhav enters*]

Madhav

Have you any idea of the trouble you've got me into, between you two?

Gaffer

What's the matter?

Madhav

I hear you've let it get rumored about that the King has planted his office here to send messages to both of you.

Gaffer

Well, what about it?

Madhav

Our headman Panchanan has had it told to the King anonymously.

Gaffer

Aren't we aware that everything reaches the King's ears?

Madhav

Then why don't you look out? Why take the King's name in vain? You'll bring me to ruin if you do.

Amal

Say, Fakir, will the King be cross?

Gaffer

Cross, nonsense! And with a child like you and a fakir such as I am. Let's see if the King be angry, and then won't I give him a piece of my mind.

Amal

Say, Fakir, I've been feeling a sort of darkness coming over my eyes since the morning. Everything seems like a dream. I long to be quiet. I don't feel like talking at all. Won't the King's letter come? Suppose this room melts away all on a sudden, suppose——

Gaffer [*Fanning Amal*]

The letter's sure to come to-day, my boy.

[*Doctor enters*]

Doctor

And how do you feel to-day?

Amal

Feel awfully well to-day, Doctor. All pain seems to have left me.

Doctor [*Aside to Madhav*]

Don't quite like the look of that smile. Bad sign that, his feeling well! Chakradhan has observed——

Madhav

For goodness sake, Doctor, leave Chakradhan alone. Tell me what's going to happen?

Doctor

Can't hold him in much longer, I fear! I warned you before—This looks like a fresh exposure.

Madhav

No, I've used the utmost care, never let him out of doors; and the windows have been shut almost all the time.

Doctor

There's a peculiar quality in the air to-day. As I came in I found a fearful draught through your front door. That's most hurtful. Better lock it at once. Would it matter if this kept your visitors off for two or three days? If someone happens to call unexpectedly—there's the back door. You had better shut this window as well, it's letting in the sunset rays only to keep the patient awake.

Madhav

Amal has shut his eyes. I expect he is sleeping. His face tells me—Oh, Doctor, I bring in a child who is a stranger and love him as my own, and now I suppose I must lose him!

Doctor

What's that? There's your headman sailing in!—What a bother! I must be going, brother. You had better stir about and see to the doors being properly fastened. I will send on a strong dose directly I get home. Try it on him—it may save him at last, if he can be saved at all. [*Exeunt Madhav and Doctor.*]

[*The Headman enters*]

Headman

Hello, urchin!——

Gaffer [*Rising hastily*]

'Sh, be quiet.

Amal

No, Fakir, did you think I was asleep? I wasn't. I can hear everything; yes, and voices far away. I feel that mother and father are sitting by my pillow and speaking to me.

[*Madhav enters*]

Headman

I say, Madhav, I hear you hobnob
with bigwigs nowadays.

Madhav

Spare me your jests, Headman, we
are but common people.

Headman

But your child here is expecting a
letter from the King.

Madhav

Don't you take any notice of him,
a mere foolish boy!

Headman

Indeed, why not! It'll beat the
King hard to find a better family!
Don't you see why the King plants his
new Post Office right before your window? Why there's a letter for you from
the King, urchin.

Amal [Starting up]

Indeed, really!

Headman

How can it be false? You're the King's chum. Here's your letter [*showing a blank slip of paper*]. Ha, ha, ha! This is the letter.

Amal

Please don't mock me. Say, Fakir, is it so?

Gaffer

Yes, my dear. I as Fakir tell you it *is* his letter.

Amal

How is it I can't see? It all looks so blank to me. What is there in the letter, Mr. Headman?

Headman

The King says, "I am calling on you shortly; you had better arrange puffed rice offerings for me.—Palace fare is quite tasteless to me now." Ha! ha! ha!

Madhav [*With folded palms*]

I beseech you, headman, don't you joke about these things——

Gaffer

Cutting jokes indeed, dare he!

Madhav

Are you out of your mind too, Gaffer?

Gaffer

Out of my mind, well then I am; I can read plainly that the King writes he will come himself to see Amal, with the state physician.

Amal

Fakir, Fakir, 'sh, his trumpet! Can't
you hear?

Headman

Ha! ha! ha! I fear he won't until
he's a bit more off his head.

Amal

Mr. Headman, I thought you were
cross with me and didn't love me. I
never could think you would fetch me
the King's letter. Let me wipe the
dust off your feet.

Headman

This little child does have an in-
stinct of reverence. Though a little
silly, he has a good heart.

Amal

It's hard on the fourth watch now,
I suppose—Hark the gong, "Dong,

dong, ding," "Dong, dong, ding." Is
the evening star up? How is it I can't
see——

Gaffer

Oh, the windows are all shut, I'll
open them.

[*A knocking outside*]

Madhav

What's that?—Who is it—what a
bother!

Voice [*From outside*]

Open the door.

Madhav

Say, Headman—Hope they're not
robbers.

Headman

Who's there?—It's Panchanan, the
headman, calls—Aren't you afraid of

the like of me? Fancy! The noise has
ceased! Panchanan's voice carries far.
—Yes, show me the biggest robbers!——

Madhav [*Peering out of the window*]

I should think the noise has ceased.
they've smashed the door.

[*The King's Herald enters*]

Herald

Our Sovereign King comes to-night!

Headman

My God!

Amal

At what hour of the night, Herald?

Herald

On the second watch.

Amal

When from the city gates my friend
the watchman will strike his gong,
"ding dong ding, ding dong ding"—
then?

Herald

Yes, then. The King sends his
greatest physician to attend on his
young friend.

State Physician enters

State Physician

What's this? How close it is here!
Open wide all the doors and windows.
[*Feeling Amal's body*] How do you feel,
my child?

Amal

I feel very well, Doctor, very well.
All pain is gone. How fresh and open!
I can see all the stars now twinkling
from the other side of the dark.

Physician

Will you feel well enough to leave your bed with the King when he comes in the middle watches of the night?

Amal

Of course, I'm dying to be about for ever so long. I'll ask the King to find me the polar star.—I must have seen it often, but I don't know exactly which it is.

Physician

He will tell you everything. [*To Madhav*] Will you go about and arrange flowers through the room for the King's visit? [*Indicating the Headman*] We can't have that person in here.

Amal

No, let him be, Doctor. He is a friend. It was he who brought me the King's letter.

Physician

Very well, my child. He may remain if he is a friend of yours.

Madhav [*Whispering into Amal's ear*]

My child, the King loves you. He is coming himself. Beg for a gift from him. You know our humble circumstances.

Amal

Don't you worry, Uncle.—I've made up my mind about it.

Madhav

What is it, my child?

Amal

I shall ask him to make me one of his postmen that I may wander far and wide, delivering his message from door to door.

Madhav [*Slapping his forehead*]

Alas, is that all?

Amal

What'll be our offerings to the King,
Uncle, when he comes?

Herald

He has commanded puffed rice.

Amal

Puffed rice! Say, Headman, you're
right. You said so. You knew all we
didn't.

Headman

If you send word to my house then I
could manage for the King's advent
really nice——

Physician

No need at all. Now be quiet all of
you. Sleep is coming over him. I'll

sit by his pillow; he's dropping into slumber. Blow out the oil-lamp. Only let the star-light stream in. Hush, he slumbers.

Madhav [*Addressing Gaffer*]

What are you standing there for like a statue, folding your palms.—I am nervous.—Say, are they good omens? Why are they darkening the room? How will star-light help?

Gaffer

Silence, unbeliever.

[*Sudha enters*]

Sudha

Amal!

Physician

He's asleep.

Sudha

I have some flowers for him.   Mayn't I give them into his own hand?

Physician

Yes, you may.

Sudha

When will he be awake?

Physician

Directly the King comes and calls him.

Sudha

Will you whisper a word for me in his ear?

Physician

What shall I say?

Sudha

Tell him Sudha has not forgotten him.

CURTAIN

A NEW PLAY

By RABINDRANATH TAGORE

Nobel Prizeman in Literature, 1913. Author of " Gitanjali,"
" The Gardener," " The Crescent Moon," " Sadhana."

CHITRA

A PLAY IN ONE ACT

Cloth, 12mo, $1.00 net; postpaid, $1.08

 This is a little lyrical drama based upon an incident in the
Mahabharata. In the course of his wanderings in fulfill-
ment of a vow of penance Arjuna comes to Manipur.
There he sees Chitrangada, the daughter of Chitravahana,
the king of the country. Smitten with her charms, he asks
the king for the hand of his daughter. Out of the king's
reply and the conditions which he imposes upon Arjuna
the story develops. It is a rare bit of idealistic writing,
as beautiful in its thought as it is in expression.

———

THE MACMILLAN COMPANY
Publishers   64-66 Fifth Avenue   New York

THE WORKS OF
RABINDRANATH TAGORE

Nobel Prizeman in Literature, 1913

GITANJALI (Song Offerings). A Collection of Prose Translations made by the author from the original Bengali $1.40 net

THE GARDENER. Poems of Youth $1.25 net

THE CRESCENT MOON. Child Poems. (Colored Ill.) $1.25 net

SADHANA: THE REALIZATION OF LIFE. A volume of essays $1.25 net

All four by Rabindranath Tagore, translated by the author from the original Bengali.

Rabindranath Tagore is the Hindu poet and preacher to whom the Nobel Prize was recently awarded. . . .

I would commend these volumes, and especially the one entitled " Sadhana," the collection of essays, to all intelligent readers. I know of nothing, except it be Maeterlinck, in the whole modern range of the literature of the inner life that can compare with them.

There are no preachers nor writers upon spiritual topics, whether in Europe or America, that have the depth of insight, the quickness of religious apperception, combined with the intellectual honesty and scientific clearness of Tagore. . . .

Here is a book from a master, free as the air, with a mind universal as the sunshine. He writes, of course, from the standpoint of the Hindu. But, strange to say, his spirit and teaching come nearer to Jesus, as we find Him in the Gospels, than any modern Christian writer I know.

He does for the average reader what Bergson and Eucken are doing for scholars; he rescues the soul and its faculties from their enslavement to logic-chopping. He shows us the way back to Nature and her spiritual voices.

He rebukes our materialistic, wealth-mad, Western life with the dignity and authority of one of the old Hebrew prophets. . . .

He opens up the meaning of life. He makes us feel the redeeming fact that life is tremendous, a worth-whiie adventure. " Everything has sprung from immortal life and is vibrating with life. LIFE IS IMMENSE." . . .

Tagore is a great human being. His heart is warm with love. His thoughts are pure and high as the galaxy.

(Copyright, 1913, by Frank Crane.) Reprinted by permission from the *New York Globe*, Dec. 18, 1913.

THE MACMILLAN COMPANY

Publishers 64-66 Fifth Avenue New York

IMPORTANT BOOKS OF POETRY

By GEORGE EDWARD WOODBERRY

THE FLIGHT AND OTHER POEMS

Cloth   12mo $1.25 net

In "The Flight and Other Poems" Dr. Woodberry has drawn his subjects mainly from his Italian and African experiences. The work expresses his mature philosophy of life and is probably the highest reach of a poet who is thought by many to stand in the front of the literary ranks of America.

By HERMANN HAGEDORN

POEMS AND BALLADS

Cloth   12mo $1.00 net

". . . It is the song that the new century needs. His verse is strong and flexible and has an ease, a naturalness, a rhythm that is rare in young poets. In many of his shorter lyrics he recalls Heine." — *Boston Transcript.*

By FANNIE STEARNS DAVIS

MYSELF AND I   *Cloth   12mo $1.00 net*

"In this first book — where every verse is significant — Miss Davis has achieved very beautiful and serious poetry." — *Boston Transcript.*

By JOHN HELSTON

APHRODITE AND OTHER POEMS

Cloth   12mo $1.25 net

This book introduces another poet of promise to the verse-lovers of this country. It is of interest to learn that Mr. Helston, who for several years was an operative mechanic in electrical works, has created a remarkable impression in England where much is expected of him. This volume, characterized by verse of rare beauty, presents his most representive work, ranging from the long descriptive title-poem to shorter lyrics.

THE MACMILLAN COMPANY

Publishers   64–66 Fifth Avenue   New York

By
WILFRID WILSON GIBSON

Daily Bread

New Edition. Three volumes in one. Cloth, 12mo.
$1.25 net.

"A Millet in word-painting who writes with a terrible simplicity is Wilfrid Wilson Gibson, born in Hexham, England, in 1878, of whom Canon Cheyne wrote: 'A new poet of the people has risen up among us.' The story of a soul is written as plainly in 'Daily Bread' as in 'The Divine Comedy' and in 'Paradise Lost.'"—*The Outlook.*

Fires

Cloth. 12mo. $1.25 net.

"In 'Fires' as in 'Daily Bread,' the fundamental note is human sympathy with the whole of life. Impressive as these dramas are, it is in their cumulative effect that they are chiefly powerful."—*Atlantic Monthly.*

Womenkind

Cloth. 12mo. $1.25 net.

"Mr. Gibson is a genuine singer of his own day and turns into appealing harmony the world's harshly jarring notes of poverty and pain."—*The Outlook.*

PUBLISHED BY

THE MACMILLAN COMPANY
64-66 Fifth Avenue   New York

A LIST OF PLAYS

Leonid Andreyev's Anathema . . . . $1.25 net
Clyde Fitch's The Climbers . . . . .75 net
    Girl with the Green Eyes . . . . 1.25 net
    Her Own Way . . . . .75 net
    Stubbornness of Geraldine . . . . .75 net
    The Truth . . . . .75 net
Thomas Hardy's The Dynasts. 3 Parts. Each . 1.50 net
Henry Arthur Jones's
    Whitewashing of Julia . . . . .75 net
    Saints and Sinners . . . . .75 net
    The Crusaders . . . . .75 net
    Michael and His Lost Angel . . . . .75 net
Jack London's Scorn of Women . . . . . . 1.25 net
    Theft . . . . 1.25 net
Mackaye's Jean D'Arc . . . . 1.25 net
    Sappho and Phaon . . . . 1 25 net
    Fenris the Wolf . . . . 1.25 net
    Mater . . . . 1.25 net
    Canterbury Pilgrims . . . . 1.25 net
    The Scarecrow . . . . 1.25 net
    A Garland to Sylvia . . . . 1.25 net
John Masefield's The Tragedy of Pompey . . . 1.25 net
William Vaughn Moody's
    The Faith Healer . . . . 1.25 net
Stephen Phillip's Ulysses . . . . 1.25 net
    The Sin of David . . . . 1.25 net
    Nero . . . . 1.25 net
    Pietro of Siena . . . . 1.00 net
Phillips and Carr. Faust . . . . 1.25 net
Edward Sheldon's The Nigger . . . . 1.25 net
    Romance . . . . 1.25 net
Katrina Trask's In the Vanguard . . . . . . 1.25 net
Rabindranath Tagore's The Post Office . . . . 1.25 net
    Chitra . . . . 1.00 net
Sarah King Wiley's Coming of Philibert . . . 1.25 net
    Alcestis . . . . .75 net
Yeat's Poems and Plays, Vol. II, Revised Edition . 2.00 net
    Hour Glass (and others) . . . . 1.25 net
    The Green Helmet and Other Poems . . . . 1.25 net
Yeats and Lady Gregory's Unicorn from the Stars 1.50 net
Israel Zangwill's The Melting Pot . . . . . . 1.25 net
    The War God . . . . 1.25 net
    The Next Religion . . . . 1.25 net

THE MACMILLAN COMPANY

Publishers   **64-66 Fifth Avenue**   **New York**